W9-AMN-635

digging

smiling

hugging

sweeping

bouncing

stamping

reading

crawling

sucking

BLOOMFIELD TOWNSHIP PUBLIC LIBRARY
1099 Lone Pine Road
Bloomfield Hills, Michigan 48302-2437

For Jack

Copyright © 1993 by Shirley Hughes

All rights reserved.

First U.S. edition 1993
First published in Great Britain in 1993 by Walker Books Ltd., London.

Library of Congress Cataloging-in-Publication Data:

Hughes, Shirley
Bouncing / Shirley Hughes.—1st U.S. ed.
Summary: A girl and her family enjoy many different kinds of bouncing.
[1. Play—Fiction.]   I. Title
PZ7.H67395Bo   1993   92-53001
[E]—dc20
ISBN 1-56402-128-9

10 9 8 7 6 5 4 3 2 1

Printed and bound in Hong Kong
by Dai Nippon Printing Co. (H.K.) Ltd.

The artwork for this book was done with colored pencils,
watercolors, and pen line.

Candlewick Press
2067 Massachusetts Avenue
Cambridge, Massachusetts 02140

Bouncing

Shirley Hughes

CANDLEWICK PRESS
CAMBRIDGE, MASSACHUSETTS

When I throw my big shiny ball . . .

it bounces away from me.

Bounce, bounce, bounce, bounce!

Then it rolls along the ground, and it stops.

I like bouncing too. In the mornings
I bounce on my bed,

and the baby bounces in his crib.

Mom and Dad's big bed is an even better
place to bounce.

But Dad doesn't like being bounced
on in the early morning.

So we roll on the floor instead, and the baby bounces on ME!

After breakfast he
does some dancing
in his baby bouncer,

and I do some dancing
to the radio.

At my play group there are big cushions on
the floor where lots of children
can bounce together.

And at home there's a big sofa where we can bounce when Mom isn't looking.

Grandpa and I know a good bouncing game.

I ride on his knees and we sing:

This is the way the ladies ride, trit-trot, trit-trot,

This is the way the gentlemen ride, giddy-up, giddy-up.

This is the way the farmers ride, clip-clop, clip-clop,

This is the way the jockeys ride, gallopy, gallopy,

and FALL OFF!

I like bouncing.

I bounce around all day...

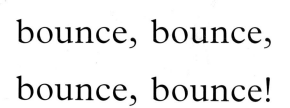

bounce, bounce,
bounce, bounce!

Until in the end I stop bouncing,

and go to sleep.

running

painting

looking

drinking

bouncing

counting

sitting

bending

scowling